Woman Walks into a Bar

Rowan Coleman worked in bookselling and then publishing for seven years, during which time she wrote her first novel, *Growing Up Twice*, published in 2002. She left to write her second novel, *After Ever After*, and now lives in Hertfordshire with her husband and daughter.

Also by Rowan Coleman

Woman Walks into a Bar

Rowan Coleman

arrow books

Published by Arrow Books in 2006

1 3 5 7 9 10 8 6 4 2

Copyright © Rowan Coleman 2006

Rowan Coleman has asserted her right under the Copyright,
Designs and Patents Act 1988 to be identified
as the author of this work

This novel is a work of fiction. Names and characters are the product
of the author's imagination and any resemblance to actual persons,
living or dead, is entirely coincidental

First published in the United Kingdom in 2006 by Arrow Books

Arrow Books
The Random House Group Limited
20 Vauxhall Bridge Road,
London SW1V 2SA

Random House Australia (Pty) Limited
20 Alfred Street, Milsons Point, Sydney,
New South Wales 2061, Australia

Random House New Zealand Limited
18 Poland Road, Glenfield,
Auckland 10, New Zealand

Random House (Pty) Limited
Isle of Houghton, Corner of Boundary Road & Carse O'Gowrie,
Houghton 2198, South Africa

The Random House Group Limited Reg. No. 954009

www.randomhouse.co.uk

A CIP catalogue record for this book is available from
the British Library

ISBN 978 0 09 949228 3 (from Jan 2007)
ISBN 0 09 949228 8

Papers used by The Random House Group Limited are natural,
recyclable products made from wood grown in sustainable forests.
The manufacturing processes conform to the environmental
regulations of the country of origin

Typeset by SX Composing DTP, Rayleigh, Essex
Printed and bound in Great Britain by
Bookmarque Limited, Croydon, Surrey

Many thanks for their help and inspiration to Jenny Main, Maggie Nutt and the Skills for Life students at Mid Essex Adult Community College. Also thank you to Kate Elton, Georgina Hawtrey-Woore, Lizzy Kremer and Philippa Hayward.

CHAPTER ONE

'YOU ARE JOKING,' I said, straight-faced. 'You had better be bloody joking.'

Joy and Marie exchanged looks over the canteen table.

'Why would we be joking?' Joy said, leaning back in her chair and patting the pocket of her jacket in search of her fags. She winked at Marie. 'Do I look like I'm joking?'

'No!' Marie replied, even though she was laughing. 'We're not joking Sam – we really have set you up on a blind date! In the White Horse – tonight at seven. Are you excited or what?' She sort of squealed and bounced up and down in her chair as she spoke. Marie is the kind of person who gets very excited over nothing much at all. I put it down to her not having any kids. If she had kids she'd be too knackered to get excited about anything. I was pissed off.

'You have *not* set me up on a blind date,' I said firmly, looking at Joy. I was trying to show her how angry I was. But in all the years I've known her I've never seen Joy afraid, least of all of me. She tipped her chin back as far as it would go and blew smoke into the air above the table because she knew that too much smoke in the air would make me need my blue inhaler. She seemed to have forgotten that stress makes me need it too.

'It'll be great,' she said, as she leant forward over the table and stubbed the butt of her fag out in a tinfoil ashtray. 'When have I ever let you down?'

I had to admit she was right. Joy had always been there for me from the first day we'd met at school until now. She was my best friend through thick and thin. Mostly thick as it turned out. Which is why she should know not to set me up on a blind date. She should know how much I'll hate it.

Joy looked at the clock on the canteen wall. 'Come on, break's nearly up and I've got to get back. Sulky Sandra wants me to re-stock feminine hygiene before dinner. Lucky me. A whole morning of stacking tampons.' She and

2

Marie started to get up but I didn't. I just sat there and stared at her. She sat down again.

'Look,' she said, starting to latch onto the idea that I was not very happy. 'It'll be a laugh! You turn up looking sexy. He'll buy you all the drinks you want and if you don't like him you can leave. OK?'

'But it's Friday night,' I said. 'It's *our* night out. Our girls' night,' I thought of our usual routine at the end of the week. Me, Joy and Marie down the White Horse every Friday night at seven. A few Bacardi Breezers to warm us up before the disco started and then we'd dance the rest of the night away. It was a stupid disco, really cheesy. But we always had a good laugh, just the three of us. It was a *girls'* night out. Just girls. Marie didn't bring her husband and Joy didn't go on the pull. And we always, always dressed up to the nines like we were going to some West End hot spot, not the local pub. Marie, tall and skinny, with her blonde curls piled high on her head so she'd tower over any man that dared to chat her up. Joy, in her latest slinky dress with all the right curves in all the right places. And me with a lot of the wrong curves in a lot of the wrong places, and hair that's just brown and eyes that are just grey, but who still – even if I say it myself – scrubs up pretty well compared to some. But now Joy had put a man right in the middle of it. It made me feel hurt, like she was trying to get rid of me. It was a stupid thought, but I get stupid thoughts like that. I have done since I was a kid. And I haven't always been wrong.

'We'll be there too,' Marie said. 'To keep an eye on you.'

'Piss yourselves laughing at me you mean,' I said, starting to feel anxious. I put my hand in my jeans pocket to check that my inhaler was there if I needed it. I didn't find my inhaler, just a small square of folded up paper. I wrapped my fingers round it and held it. 'Anyway, Joy, I know all the blokes you know. You wouldn't go out with any of them – what makes you think I would?'

Joy leant over the table and put her hand on mine. It was cold. Joy always had cold hands. 'Cold hands, warm heart,' she always said. And most of the time it was true.

'We'll be there to keep an eye on you, idiot,' she said, smiling at me. 'We don't want you to get in any more trouble do we? Think of Marie and me as your bodyguards. Hanging about in the background. You won't know we're there unless you need us. And then we'll be like Pow! Pow!' Joy chopped her hand through the air as she spoke but I shook my head.

'No,' I said. 'Look, you'll have to phone this bloke up and tell him no. All right? I'm not going on a blind date!' I leant back in the chair and crossed my arms. 'Blind dates are for sad bastards who can't meet people in a normal way.'

Joy and Marie laughed. I knew why they were laughing and I supposed it was pretty funny. I felt the corners of my mouth twitch but I made them stay down. I didn't want to stop being angry until this whole thing was cleared up.

'So Internet dating isn't like a blind date then?' Marie said, her mouth curled into a smile.

'No,' I said, rolling my eyes like my daughter Beth would have. 'You know a lot about the person before you meet them and they know a lot about you. And you've seen a photo.'

'Yeah, but whose photo!' Joy cried, slapping the palm of her hand down on the table as she spoke. She and Marie were laughing again.

'You know what?' I said, only half angry now. 'Everyone thinks my love life is such a joke. And I reckon I must be the punch line because I tell

5

you what, everyone else but me thinks it's funny!'

'What was his name again, the one who sent someone else's photo?' Joy asked me, between laughs.

'Bill, and it wasn't someone else's photo – it was his photo,' I said, feeling the corners of my mouth start to twitch again. 'Just one he'd had taken twenty years before, that's all.'

And then we were all laughing.

The One Who Was All Right Really But Not for Me

I walked into the bar.

It wasn't the usual sort of place I'd go to. It was a wine bar in the town centre. Beth said I needed to wear a skirt and put my hair up, but my hair is quite fine so it had taken half a can of hairspray to get it to stay put. It felt like I had a Brillo pad on my head. It made me walk like I had a stiff neck.

I had his photo in my bag. Beth had printed it off for me. Underneath it she had written one of the jokes from *The 1001 Worst Jokes Ever* book my mum had given her for Christmas. She pretended she was too old to find the jokes funny any more, but she'd read them out to me so we could laugh at how un-funny they were. She'd started writing jokes out on slips of paper and leaving them in surprise places for me to find, like in my purse or knicker drawer.

A horse walked into a bar and the barman said, 'Why the long face?'

I smiled at the joke, not because it was funny but because it made me happy to know that Beth wanted me to do this. It gave me courage.

We thought Bill's face looked nice. The right one for my first date in nearly eight years. Twinkly eyes, friendly smile and dark, wavy hair. But it took me a while to recognise him because most of the wavy hair had gone. And the nice eyes had gone from twinkly to wrinkly. And the friendly smile was perched on top of at least three more chins than were in his photo.

'Samantha!' he said, walking towards me stretching out his hand. He shook it hard so that the fat on the top of my arm wobbled. 'You look just like your photo. Pretty as a picture.' I smiled at him but I didn't know what to say. He reminded me of my dad.

I thought as I was in a wine bar I'd better have wine, but I didn't drink much of it. It tasted sour and seemed to make my mouth feel drier with every sip. We sat on two bar stools at a high, round table. He kept slipping off his.

He talked, I listened. At first I had thought he was pretty funny and sad. A funny, sad man trying to fool women into going out with him with his old photo. But then I started to listen to what he said and I realised there was nothing really wrong with him. He was a nice man, a nice, lonely man. I liked him. I had even decided it would be too cruel to say no to a second date. That I'd agree now and then just ring him later with a really good excuse. Like I'd died or something.

A few times he reached out and covered my hand with the hot and heavy weight of his, so that I'd be forced to pick up my wine glass and take another sip of it so I could free my fingers from his damp grasp. But it wasn't like he was trying to touch me. He just wanted someone to hold on to. I knew how that felt.

'You're a good listener, Samantha,' he said, suddenly getting teary. 'I really like you. You're a fine-looking woman. But I'm sorry, I shouldn't be leading you on like this. I shouldn't be here at all!'

'Funny,' I said, lightly. 'That's just what I was thinking!'

'I can't love you, Sam,' he said, without hearing me.

'Not to worry,' I said.

'No, no – don't try and talk me round. It wouldn't be love between us, you see. It would just be sex and you deserve more. Much more than just *animal lust*.' His chins wobbled when he got worked up.

'Thanks,' I said. I took a big gulp of the wine and didn't care what it tasted like.

'It's not you,' he said. 'It's me. I still love her you see? I still love her, and I can't get her out of my head. I've tried! Oh God, I've tried! But the first cut is the deepest isn't it?'

I nodded.

'You're a lovely girl, Samantha,' he said. 'And that's why I must be honest. It's not going to work out between us. I'm sorry.'

*

9

And that was how I got dumped less than one hour into my first ever Internet date by a man twice my age with practically no hair.

It might have put some people off for good. But 'some people' didn't have my daughter to contend with.

CHAPTER TWO

IT HAD BEEN BETH's idea to join me up on an Internet dating agency about six months ago. I would never have thought about joining any kind of dating agency let alone one on the Internet, but to Beth it seemed as normal as breathing.

'I'm twelve, Mum,' she said. 'I'll be grown up soon. It's about time you got a boyfriend while you're still quite thin.' I'd started to say no way but when I thought about it I realised that she was right, in a way. It only seemed like yesterday that she was a baby crawling around on the kitchen tiles and now here she was in her first bra, nicking my eyeliner.

For a long time, years after I broke up with my ex, Adam, I didn't think about having a boyfriend at all. I couldn't face the thought of it. But then a while back I started remembering what it feels like. To have a man's warmth lying in bed next to me, or to have someone hold my hand and kiss me. Not just hugs and kisses like I used to get from Beth all the time until she started feeling so grown up, but kisses that mean something. Touches that made me feel *something* inside. That made me feel like I was more than just awake. That made me feel like I was alive too.

For a long time just thinking about any of those things had made me feel angry and frightened, but lately I'd been thinking how nice it would be to go to sleep with someone's arms around me apart from my own.

Beth made me sit on her bed while she filled in my details on the computer my brother had got her last Christmas, even though she didn't ask me once what to write. She just talked aloud as she typed stuff in.

'Five foot, six, slim build, blue eyes, blonde hair, likes . . .' She'd turned and looked me up and down, '. . . music, theatre, films, eating out and good times. I'll send this picture Uncle Eddie took of you at New Year. The one before you were drunk and still had lipstick on.'

I had thought about pointing out that I wasn't quite that tall, that I didn't think a size sixteen counted as slim, that my eyes were grey, my hair was more of a light brown and that really my idea of a good time was a night in with the telly and a bar of Dairy Milk. But while I was thinking about it she had clicked around with that mouse thing and all the stuff she had typed was sent. Sent where and how I had no idea. But some place where other people could look at it.

'I'm not sure,' I'd said, feeling my chest tighten as Beth turned off the Internet and started fishing about in her school bag for her homework. I'd fished in my pocket for my blue inhaler. 'I mean, can you get it back? I've changed my mind.'

Beth had rolled her eyes at me. She does that a lot these days.

'Mum,' she'd said. 'You're twenty-eight. You're younger than Posh Spice, even if you don't look it. You need a boyfriend. This will be great, trust me. Everyone does it these days. Miss Porter did and now she's getting married!' I'd sat there for a moment longer watching her using the computer like she'd been born to use it, until she'd rolled her eyes again and said, 'Mu-um! Go and watch *EastEnders* or something, *please*!'

13

I had had three responses from the agency so far. I had been on three dates. And they were blind dates I suppose because, honestly, there was no way I saw any of that lot coming.

CHAPTER THREE

JUST BEFORE GETTING BACK to work I unfolded the square of paper in my jeans pocket and read the joke that Beth had left for me.

How do you know when you've got an elephant in your fridge?
There are footprints in the butter!

I groaned but couldn't help laughing. That one was pretty funny, if you had the mentality of a four-year-old. Joy found it hilarious.

'Get a move on, girls!' Sandra bellowed across the canteen at us. 'Break was over five minutes ago!'

The three of us stood up and started to make our way back to the shop floor. Marie first, then me, followed by Joy trailing behind. Joy was complaining because she was on tampons.

'I wish I was on tampons,' I said to her over

my shoulder. 'I'm on fresh fish. I hate fresh fish, it makes me want to gag.'

'Marie,' Joy called out as we filed out of the canteen. 'You've got to get her off fresh fish. We don't want her stinking of fish guts tonight, do we?'

Marie was the shift checkout captain. Or Captain Checkout as Joy called her. Marie loved herself in her special orange blazer, tottering up and down the tills with her clipboard.

'I'll have a word with Sandra,' she said, slightly on the snooty side. Marie took her job very seriously. Checkout captain wasn't enough for her. She had her eye on section manager tomorrow and assistant manager the day after that. And the day after that, Joy often teased her, the world.

Joy, on the other hand, treated her job at the supermarket exactly the same way she had treated school. She looked upon it as a way to have as much of a laugh as you could without getting put into detention. That was why she was never checkout captain.

I was never checkout captain because I couldn't work a till without killing it. Even the modern ones where you just have to put the barcode under a red light and the till reads it for you. It's not because I don't know how they work, I do. But I always seem to make electric things go wrong. I only have to look at them.

Whenever I'm on a till it always gets jammed or broken within about ten minutes. It's always on a Saturday morning. There's always a huge queue and it's always some arsey woman I'm holding up, tapping her credit card like fury on the counter because she'll be a few minutes late picking her kid up from ballet in her car which is the size of a bus. And when people start to look at me like I'm stupid, I start feeling stupid and all of the things I know I should do to put the till right go out of my head. I look at it but it's like I'm looking at something I have never seen before in my life. It makes no sense to me. So then I have to flash my light until the checkout captain comes over and presses two buttons to make it work again. And then I get sent on a break and when I come back I'm back on fresh fish.

So I only ever get out on the till when there's been flu going around or on Valentine's Day when no one else wants to work in the evening.

Joy treats her job like a laugh, Marie treats it

like a career path and I treat it exactly like what it is. A way to support myself and Beth. A way to get her the latest pair of trainers or games for the Xbox my brother bought her, without having to answer to anyone but myself.

I'm luckier than some. Mum and Dad do pretty well – Dad's garage makes good money. I know he'd help us more with money if I let him. He tells me so every time we go round there for fish and chips on a Wednesday night. And I know Beth thinks I should let him, that a bit more cash would be a quicker route to whatever skirt, top or DVD she wants – but I won't let him.

When Adam left I had to pick myself up and get on with things. I had to look after myself and my daughter. I had to do it for myself to prove that I could be strong. And sometimes it's hard but I want to do it by myself, and whenever I look around everything we've got I know that it's almost all because of me and I'm really proud.

CHAPTER FOUR

'DON'T GET ME MOVED off fresh fish,' I said to Marie. 'I'm not going to meet this bloke, remember?'

Marie sighed and picked up her clipboard.

'Oh come on, Sam,' she pleaded. 'You're never going to believe who it is!'

I blinked at her. That meant I knew whoever it was they were trying to set me up with.

'Marie!' Joy scowled at her. 'We're not telling her who it is, all right?'

'I haven't told her who it is! All I've said is . . .'

'What, I know this person?' I said, looking at Joy.

'Yeah,' Joy said, looking a bit awkward.

'I know him and he's not one of your cast-offs?'

Joy nodded.

I looked at Marie. 'Who is he, Marie?' I asked.

'I'm not telling,' Marie said, 'but when you see him you'll be well glad you went, I promise you . . .'

A list of all the people I thought it might be flashed through my head in a split second.

'Brian?' I asked.

'No,' Joy replied.

'Mick, Dave, Jules, Ali . . . ?'

Joy and Maria shook their heads on each name and I was glad. I didn't want it to be any of those names. But if it wasn't any of them and it was someone that I knew, who did that leave?

I thought of a name but I didn't say it out loud.

There was one person who I'd like to see sitting at the table waiting to buy me a drink at seven p.m. that night. But it couldn't be that person for two reasons. Firstly, neither Joy nor Marie nor anyone on earth except me knew that I liked him. And secondly he was the bar manager at the White Horse. He'd be there to see me meeting up with whoever this geek was because he was bound to be working on a Friday night. Wasn't he?

I hadn't started out fancying Brendan. It wasn't

like the first time I saw him I couldn't speak and my heart was racing and I knew I was in love. He didn't blow me away exactly. In fact, I thought he was a bit too short for me and he was very quiet at first, shy. Marie was the first to notice he had nice eyes and Joy liked his Irish accent.

He'd been working at the White Horse for a few months before I realised that the person I most looked forward to seeing on a Friday night was not Joy or Marie. It was him. I'd been getting ready to meet the girls as usual when I realised my belly felt funny. Sort of twisted. I thought it might have been the Chicken Tikka sandwich I had had for lunch so I went and sat on the loo but nothing happened. It reminded me of something I had felt before, and I remembered the first time I had felt Beth moving inside me, fluttering against my insides like a bird beating its wings. But I couldn't be pregnant.

And then I laughed out loud sitting on the loo. It had been so long since I had had that feeling I'd forgotten it altogether. It was butterflies! It was the thought of seeing Brendan that night that was making me feel excited. I'd probably fancied him for ages before that night. It just took me a long time to realise it. I had thought that those sorts of feelings inside me had gone forever. I thought they had been kicked to death.

But I didn't tell anyone. Because if Joy found out the world would have known by tea time. And because Brendan wasn't going to fancy someone like me, not when he had skinny twenty-year-olds throwing themselves at him every night of the week. And because while nobody knew, and it was just my secret, I could hold it close inside and enjoy it and pretend that it might be real one day.

I looked at Joy and then another thought of who it might be swept over me and I found myself shaking. I must have gone white because Joy reached out an arm to steady me and took a step closer.

'Babe,' she said gently. 'What?'

I made myself ask.

'It's not . . . it's not *him* is it,' I asked in a whisper. The laughter in Joy's face was gone in an instant.

'Sam, no! No. I would never, *never* do that, you know that,' Joy told me firmly.

'I know you wouldn't mean to,' I said. 'But

22

you know what he's like. I thought if he wanted to see me he'd try and talk you round and maybe . . . maybe . . . maybe.' My words had got stuck, like a scratch on a CD. Only talking about Adam did that to me. I don't know what would happen if I actually saw him.

'Listen to me,' Joy said, putting her other hand on my shoulder. 'It's not him. He doesn't even live round here any more. And he'd never come back here. He knows what would happen to him if he did. It's not him, OK?' I nodded and Joy bit her lip as she looked at me.

'I hate it when you're like this, Sam,' she said. 'When are you going to realise no one can hurt you now? You are a strong independent woman, all right? And anyway I'm here, your mum and dad, Eddie . . .'

'And me,' Marie said, feeling left out.

'For what's it's worth,' Joy said, winking at me. 'He's *gone*. He's been gone for years. He's never coming back. It's not him. You have to stop letting him frighten you.'

I nodded and took a deep breath. I felt in my other pocket and found my inhaler and took two puffs. Deep breath, count to ten. Deep breath, count to ten.

'Do you need to go sick?' Sandra snapped too loudly in my ear.

'No, Sandra,' I said. 'Just a bit wheezy . . .'

'Well, stop standing around gossiping and get on with it then, all right? This is not a holiday camp!' We watched her arse wobble as she marched off towards canned goods.

'Look, just be there tonight, OK?' Joy said. 'You'll be glad that you did.' She was smiling again.

I thought for a moment. If it wasn't any of the people I didn't want it to be then there was a chance, a small chance, that it might be Brendan.

Beth's always telling me that if I start thinking good things will happen to me then they will. She says, 'There's no point in moaning about not winning the lottery, Mum, when you don't ever buy a ticket. You can't expect the right bloke just to turn up right under your nose. You have to go out and find him. You have to take chances.'

It probably wouldn't be Brendan that I was going to meet as my blind date in the bar tonight. But there was a chance it might be. A chance worth taking.

24

'All right,' I said, finding myself smiling as the butterflies kicked off in my guts again. 'Why not?'

'Hooray!' Marie cheered quietly, as she slotted her pen into the top of her clipboard. 'And at least he's got to be better than that twat you met at Roxy's,' she said.

'Oh yeah?' I asked. 'Why?'

'He's not married,' she said.

The One Who Was No Good for Any Woman Including His Wife

I walked into the bar.

I hadn't been to Roxy's in years. And now I remembered why. The thump of the music made my ears ring and the flash of the lights made me squint. I don't know why this Graham had picked a nightclub on a Thursday night for us to meet. It was only just eight and the place was more or less empty. The air conditioning made me get goose bumps on my arms and the dry ice made me cough. I unfolded the email that Beth had printed off for me with instructions on where we were to meet.

25

'Upstairs in the booths,' it read. I looked at his photo. Even in the pulsing strobe lights he was pretty good looking. Beth had written out a joke underneath the photo.

What does Dracula say to his victims?
It's been nice gnawing you!

I smiled. The joke wasn't funny. But Beth going to the trouble to do something to make me smile when I was feeling nervous made me happy. Sometimes I wondered how, despite everything, I had ended up with such a great kid.

When I walked up the stairs the noise of the music went down a little bit. All of the booths seemed to be empty but I walked along the row from one to another until I found him, sitting in the corner. He had been watching himself in the mirrored wall and turned round when he saw my reflection.

'There you are,' he said. I wondered if he was talking to me or my chest.

'Here I am,' I said, feeling nervous. 'Ha ha.'

He patted the seat next to him for me to sit down. I did. He pushed a drink towards me across the table. It was tall with lots of ice in it, a curly straw and an umbrella stuck in the top.

'I got you a cocktail,' he said. 'Sex on the Beach.' He looked pretty pleased with himself so I took a sip. It tasted of Ribena.

'Cheers,' I said.

He looked at my chest again and I began to wish that I hadn't let Beth talk me into buying a new top.

'You can't wear that old-lady stuff to a nightclub, Mum,' she'd said in Topshop. 'How about this one? It's in the sale.'

I hadn't liked it because it was too tight and you could see the little lumps of fat that bulged out under my bra. But Beth said it was 'way cool' so I bought it.

'Tell me about yourself, Sam,' Graham said. I didn't know what to say. No one had said that to me in years. Or maybe even ever.

'Not much to tell,' I said, sucking the cocktail through the curly straw. 'I've got a daughter called Beth who's twelve. I work at the local supermarket – that's it really. Just what it says on my thingy. Profile.'

Graham leant a bit closer to me. He smelt of strong aftershave.

'That's not what I mean,' he said, very quietly, so quietly that I had to lean closer to him to hear him above the music. 'Tell me what makes you tick.'

It was funny really because the more of the cocktail I drank the more I had to say. I ended up telling him a lot about myself. The words just seemed to tumble out. Once I got started I couldn't shut up. I didn't tell him everything, thank God. Just about what life was like for me and Beth on our own. By the end of the cocktail I found myself telling him I was lonely.

'A beautiful woman like you,' he said, 'is bound to have needs a man like me could take care of.'

'Needs?' I said, remembering that I needed to pay the gas bill as the red one had come that morning.

'Needs,' he said. And he kissed me. I was a bit taken aback at first. It took my brain a few seconds to work out what my body was doing and by that time my body was well up for it.

I was kissing him back. His hand was up my top, squeezing and groping and my hand was on his thigh. His mouth was all over mine and, as we kissed, the edges of the booth seemed to

28

blur and spin. I remember looking at my watch and being surprised that it was not even nine yet. After a bit, he broke off the kiss and wiped the back of his hand across his mouth.

'Shall we go back to your place?' he said.

'My place?' I said, thinking about my mum and Beth.

'Yeah,' he said. He reached out his left hand and traced a finger down the deep V of my top. Not just any finger. His ring finger. With a faint white band of skin around it. Skin that wouldn't have caught the sun like the rest of him because it was usually protected by a ring. I looked at the mark until I realised what it meant.

'You're married,' I said, not angry, just surprised. Graham looked at the finger too, then, and snatched it back. I think he swore under his breath, angry that I'd noticed it.

'Um, no . . .' he said. 'Well, not really. I mean, in name only. We're getting divorced in a few months . . . so come on, what do you say? What we've got is special, isn't it?'

I looked at him and thought about how he had made me feel with his hand up my top and his mouth everywhere. For a moment I thought

29

that I had wanted him but now I just felt cheap, cut-price just like my bargain-bin top.

'I'm sorry,' I said. 'I don't go with married men.' And I stood up.

'You slapper,' he said.

'What did you say?' I asked him. Normally I would have pretended I hadn't heard him, anything to avoid trouble. But I think the cocktail made me feel brave.

'I said, you fucking slapper.' He spat the words out loud enough to be clear over the music. 'I know your type. Grown-up kid at your age. You've been shagging since you were a kid, handing it out to anyone. Don't tell me that a slapper like you won't go with me because I'm married. What is it? Do you want paying?'

I wanted to answer back, to stand up for myself and make him take back everything he'd just said but I couldn't do any of those things. Not even the drink made me that brave. I'd been there before, standing in front of people with their faces full of hate, shouting insults at me. I knew there was only one thing I could do. So I just walked away as quickly as I could, pulling my coat across my chest as I walked out of the club.

As I was leaving a bouncer nodded at me.

'Good for you love,' he said. 'Lucky escape. He's got a different poor cow in here every week.'

When I got in I told Beth he wasn't for me and she just shrugged and smiled and made me a hot chocolate.

'Never mind, Mum,' she said. 'Let's log on now and see if you've got any messages.' I didn't have the heart to say no, but I cried for a long time before I went to sleep that night. And the next day at work I made it into one big joke, until Joy and Marie were laughing so much *they* were crying, and thinking about it didn't hurt any more.

CHAPTER FIVE

Deodorant
Razors
Nail varnish remover
Nail varnish
Condoms!!!

I STOOD BY THE CONDOM counter and glanced about to see if anyone was looking at me. I hadn't bought any condoms in years. I have never actually used one. There have only been two blokes. Luke Goddard, a boy I used to like from school, and that was only the once, and Adam, Beth's so-called dad. Adam didn't like using condoms so I went on the pill. It's funny. I kept taking it for nearly two years after we split up. I don't know why, routine I suppose.

And I don't know why I wrote condoms on my shopping list except Beth had been on at me to get some.

'You need to practise safe sex, Mum,' she'd told me. 'It's not just about getting pregnant you know, there's all sorts of nasty diseases around too.' We were in the kitchen at the time. She was washing up and I was peeling potatoes. I nearly took the top of my finger off.

'How do you know about condoms?' I'd said, whirling round and pointing the peeler at her.

'What do you mean, how do I know?' She'd said, without looking up from the dishes. 'I learnt about them at school. Sex education, Mum? Duh!'

I'd stopped and tried to find the right words to say. It felt like I had been waiting for her to be this age since she was born. Waiting and worrying that, as soon as she stopped playing with her Barbie and started thinking about lads, she'd go and throw everything she had away on some boy who wouldn't give a toss about her afterwards. Beth was different from me. When I fell pregnant I didn't have anything apart from my baby. I didn't have any exams. I'd left school before I could take them. I didn't have any boyfriend. I didn't have any future, not like her. She could do anything with her life. Maybe even go to college if I save enough money every month.

'Beth,' I'd said. She'd looked up from the washing up. 'I love you. You're the best thing in my life. You always will be.'

'I know,' she'd said, and blew a soap sud at me.

'But I don't want you to think that just because . . . just because I had you on my own when I was quite young that it's easy . . .'

'Mu-um!' Beth had protested. 'Honestly! No way would I ever get pregnant! What, do you think because I know about condoms I'll get pregnant or do sex? It's when you *don't* know about condoms you get pregnant! If anyone should know that, it's you.' Beth wrinkled up her nose. 'Yuck! No way am I doing sex, not for ages and ages. And anyway, even if I did I wouldn't do it without a condom.'

'But boys can put pressure on you . . .' I'd started.

'Boys are stupid, so I'm not exactly going to listen to *them* am I?' Beth had said across me. 'And I don't want you to get pregnant either. So if you want to do sex when you get a boyfriend you'd better get some condoms, OK?'

'OK,' I'd said. And then I'd decided to mash the potatoes instead of chip them.

I looked at the rest of the items I already had in my basket and decided to leave the condoms. I don't know what I was thinking even writing them on my list. What Beth didn't know was that I sometimes wondered if I'd ever have sex with any man again. Sometimes at night just as I'm drifting off to sleep I think of what it might be like with Brendan. But that's just dreaming, and anyway it probably wouldn't be Brendan waiting for me in the White Horse. So I left the condoms behind and went to the Ten Items or Less till with my discount card.

'I hear you're on a promise then, Sam?' Cathy the girl behind the till asked me with a wink. 'Haven't you forgotten something?'

I looked at my shopping and frowned.

'Oh, yeah,' I said. 'Fish fingers.'

CHAPTER SIX

BETH LEFT ME A JOKE on the front door of the flat scrawled in pink ink on a Post-it note she'd stuck down with extra tape to stop it blowing away.

'Knock knock . . .'
'Who's there?'
'Alison!'
'Alison who?'
'Alison to my teacher!!'

I read the joke twice when I got inside but I still didn't get it.

'You in?' I called.

'Yeah,' Beth called back from her bedroom. I nodded. I was always glad to hear her voice. Always glad to know that she was safe and well and had made it through another day at school without anything happening to change or hurt her.

Beth never thought about school like I did, of course. She greeted every day with the same energy and joy. She never thought that the day would come when someone wouldn't like her. Not because she'd done anything wrong but just because of who she was. She had scraps and fights with her friends but she'd never dream that the girls she'd known since playgroup would suddenly decide to turn on her one day and make her life a misery.

'That's because Beth is not you,' I had to remind myself almost every day. 'She's a strong, popular girl. She's not the sort of girl who gets bullied. She's not you.'

I paused outside Beth's door for a moment, deciding whether or not I should tell her about the date. I didn't *have* to.

As far as she was concerned I always went out on a Friday night. My mum always came over at about six and the three of us gossiped while I got ready. For the last few months Beth's best mate, Keisha, would come over just after I'd gone, to watch DVDs and eat Maltesers. I knew it would only be a matter of time before Beth herself was getting ready to go out on a Friday night and I would have a whole load of new reasons to be scared for her.

I didn't *have* to tell her about the blind date and part of me dreaded the thought of it. I'd never liked to compare her to her father, not at all, but if I had to say they had one thing in common it would be an unshakable belief that they were always right. Beth disapproved of Joy and all of her life choices, and she would disapprove of Joy setting me up for a date. Even so, I wanted to tell her, and not just because she'd kill me if she ever found out I'd kept it from her. But also because Beth was as good a friend to me as Joy or Marie. Because although I am the mum, she has always been the glue that has held me together.

I pushed open her bedroom door. She was lying on her stomach on her bed, her feet in the air.

'Doing your homework?' I asked her.

'Nope,' she looked at me over her shoulder and held up a copy of *heat* 'I think false boobs look stupid, don't you, Mum?' I shrugged and came into the room and sat down at her desk.

'I suppose so,' I said.

'Like someone's stuffed two big balloons up your top that might go pop any minute!' Beth said, holding up a picture of a bleached blonde who did look a bit overstretched, before looking down her own top.

'Joy and Marie have set me up on a blind date tonight,' I said quickly, in a low voice.

'A blind date!' Beth sat up on her bed, her eyes popping. 'Who with? How do we know if he's OK if we haven't looked him up on the Internet? What's his name?'

'I don't know,' I said smiling. 'That's why it's called a blind date.'

'Mum!' Beth protested. 'You can't just go and meet some bloke you don't know. Anything could happen!'

I sighed and tried to sound like I was the adult here.

'I do know that, Beth. Anything could happen with some bloke I meet off your computer, too. You read about it all the time in the paper.'

Beth screwed her mouth into a knot. I knew she was angry, not because I was risking life and limb by meeting a potential axe murderer for a drink, but because it had not been her idea.

'Well,' she said, 'I just hope you're meeting him in a public place. And you'd better tell at least two people where you'll be and call me when you get there . . .'

'I'm meeting him in the White Horse,' I interrupted her, before she could tell me I have to be in by nine. 'And Joy and Marie and everyone else from round here will be there too. So I don't think you have to worry, OK?' I thought about Brendan and felt a little fizz in my belly. 'It'll probably be rubbish anyway,' I said, to calm myself down.

'Bound to be if Joy's picked him,' Beth said. 'Her boyfriends are always right mingers.'

'Beth!' I said sharply. 'I don't like you using words like that!'

'It's just a word, Mum,' Beth snapped at me. 'I don't even know why you hang out with Joy. She looks a right state in those clothes that don't fit her! At your age you should . . .'

'Beth!' My raised voice stopped her in her tracks. 'Don't you ever speak about Joy or any- one like that again,' I told her. 'Joy has been a good friend to me. She has always been there – if it hadn't been for Joy after your father did . . .'

'Did what? Did what, Mum?' Beth shouted at me and I knew I shouldn't have mentioned Adam. 'What's this, what's *anything* got to do

41

with him!' She drew in a ragged breath and I knew she was trying not to cry. I know she misses the dad she can hardly remember. She doesn't say it, but I know she hates him for not being around. And sometimes I think she hates me for keeping him away. But it's hard to explain to her the reason why I do without making her hate us both even more.

I sat down on the bed next to her.

'This is stupid,' I said. 'I don't want to fall out with you. I just wish you wouldn't be so down on Joy, OK? She's a good person. The best.'

We sat in silence for a moment until the tension faded.

'I'm sorry, Mum,' Beth said. She put her arms round my neck and kissed me. She was wearing the perfume my mum had given me at Christmas. I decided not to mention it.

'So what are you going to wear to this blind date?' she said after a moment, wrinkling her nose. 'I tell you what, you'd better have a bath and wash your hair, anyway. You stink of fish.'

CHAPTER SEVEN

BETH RAN THE BATH so that the bubbles rose over the rim like mountains of soft white snow.

'What do you think of this?' Beth asked me, sitting on the loo leafing through her joke book as I shaved my legs.

'Who does a monster ask for a date?'

I waited.

'Any old ghoul he can find!' Beth screwed up her mouth.

'Worst yet,' I told her, groaning.

'Totally!' she agreed with a giggle that reminded me of when she had been very small.

'So how was school today?' I asked her, my heart in my mouth.

'Cool,' Beth said, like she always did.

'Cool how?' I pressed her like I always did, watching her carefully for any signs that she might be hiding something.

'Well, my team won at football, I got a "B" for

my history homework and we had a right laugh at lunch because Keisha fancies this lad in the year above so we spent all break trying to find him so she could ask him out and then when we did she totally bottled it! And after dinner Miss Childs said we're going to be doing *Grease* as the school play – but, Mum, it's not fair because all the sixth formers get the best parts, right? And all we'll get to do is paint scenery or something, so I said . . .'

I let Beth's words wash over me, as warm and as comforting as the bath water. Everything she was telling me now she had told me before in one way or another. It was normal for her. It was amazing to me.

My average day at school had not been the same, at least from the year I turned thirteen. That's when the bullying started.

I didn't notice it at first. It took me until break to realise that no one was talking to me. When I went up to Christine Parker and Hannah Milton as usual both of them turned their backs on me and walked away without saying a word. I wanted to run after them and ask them what I'd done wrong. But I didn't. I wasn't the sort of person to be pushy. I thought I'd wait until they were OK with me again, then say sorry for whatever it was. But at dinner they ignored me again. At home time I didn't bother trying to talk to them. I just walked right past them towards the school gate.

'Stuck up bitch thinks she's too good for us,' Hannah said. I stopped in my tracks.

'I don't !' I said, smiling. 'I just thought you didn't want to talk to me . . .'

'We don't want to talk to you, bitch,' Christine said. 'Who'd want to talk to a stinking fat bitch like you?' And they walked off, laughing and nudging each other. A couple of other kids who had heard them were laughing too.

I didn't say anything to Mum when I got home. We had fallen out before, the three of us. Sometimes it was me and Christine against Hannah. Sometimes me and Hannah against Christine. Now it was those two against me. I told myself everything would be back to normal in a couple of days, like always.

But it wasn't. It was the same for the rest of the week. And by the beginning of the next week it wasn't only Christine and Hannah that were saying things, calling me a bitch or telling

45

me I stank. It was my whole class. The week after that it seemed like it was everyone in my year. I would be walking down a corridor and someone would shove me against a wall, but when I looked round everyone was acting like nothing had happened. Little things like that, every day.

There was one time when we were getting changed for PE. Someone squeezed a packet of tomato ketchup all over my white shorts. Our PE teacher was a hard old cow. She didn't like excuses. I had to do cross country in my pants.

I had to tell my mum about that. She was livid, because the shorts were ruined. As she scrubbed at them in the sink she told me that the girls that were picking on me were just jealous of me because I was growing up so good looking. She told me to ignore them and they'd soon get bored.

But they didn't get bored. For the rest of that year they found new names to call me, new ways to torment me. And it wasn't just the girls, it was the boys too. I was one of the first in my year to wear a bra. The boys were always trying to ping the straps or grab my top and yank it down. They thought that because I was quite big up top I should be up for it. Like the size of my chest made me a tart all by itself.

And I never really knew why it happened. I never knew if I'd done anything wrong or offended someone so badly that the rest of my year slowly turned against me one by one. It felt like a tide of hate slowly building and rolling towards me day after day a little bigger each time. And there was nothing I could do. I had no idea why they had decided to hate me, single me out. And sometimes I wondered if there was any reason at all. I hope that there was because otherwise – otherwise it's too painful to think about.

So I went off sick and bunked off whenever I thought I'd get away with it.

When the summer holidays came I lay on the living-room floor with the curtains drawn and watched telly for six weeks. I hadn't wanted to go back in September. I begged Mum to let me stay at home, but she wasn't having it.

'You're not going to let a few little girls scare you off, are you, Samantha?' she asked me firmly. 'You've got to be strong to survive in this life, my girl. You can deal with this.'

She meant well, I know that. And if I'd really

told her how bad it was for me she would have done something to make it better. But I never told her. I never told anyone.

I was so scared the day I went back. But on the first day of the new year nobody paid any attention to me at all because there was a new girl in class. Joy.

Back then there weren't that many black kids at school, not many black people in the town at all. Having a black girl start in our year was sort of an occasion. It's different now. Beth's mates are all different shades and none of them see the colour of each other's skin. They just see a friend.

But when Joy started school she was different. You might have thought it would have been Joy that the bullies would pick on, but no. Everyone wanted to hang out with Joy. She had this kind of natural confidence that made you want to look at her. And she had the whole class laughing right from the first day she started. For a week or two, while Joy was the centre of attention, nobody even looked at me. I hoped that they had forgotten me completely.

And then one dinner Joy was standing by the

lockers with some of the other girls, including Hannah.

'Here she comes,' Hannah said. 'Slapper of the year. I can smell her from here.' Everyone in the group laughed, except for Joy.

'Don't speak to her like that,' she said.

Hannah took a step back. 'We're only having a laugh,' she said, looking at me. 'She's used to it, aren't you, slapper?' Joy gave Hannah a little shove so that she took another step back.

'I said, don't talk to Sam like that,' Joy said. I couldn't believe that Joy was sticking up for me. I don't think I had heard another kid use my real name for months.

'What's your problem?' Hannah said, her voice a bit shaky.

'You're my problem. I don't like the way you're talking to her,' Joy said. 'She's a person too, you know.' Hannah's jaw just dropped.

Joy turned to me and put her arm through mine. 'Come on,' she said. 'Let's get away from these losers.'

'Yeah, well, you should just go back where you came from!' Hannah called after us.

'What, Kensal Green?' Joy shouted over her shoulder and laughed.

The bullying was worse after that but somehow it didn't matter. With Joy by my side we stuck it out together. I still got that feeling of dread in the pit of my belly whenever I left the house every morning, but Joy would be waiting for me at the end of the path, by the gate. And, even though they had even worse names for her than they did for me, she'd always laugh it off and have something much funnier and more cruel to say back.

By the time Joy and me were fifteen we were used to the idea that while we were at school we would always be outsiders. Never invited to the girls' parties, never asked out by the boys. But we always said we didn't care. We said we were just waiting until the time when we'd be free of school for good, when we would really start living our lives. Then we would show them.

The beginning of GCSE year at school started out OK, just because Joy was my friend. I even stopped feeling frightened and started feeling almost normal, if not accepted. I stood up tall again and stopped trying to hide my boobs under my arms. I spoke up in class. I let myself laugh out loud when Joy was being funny. I really thought that I'd come through the worst and that everything was going to be all right.

But all of that changed after everyone found out that I'd had sex with Luke Goddard.

CHAPTER EIGHT

'DON'T SCREW YOUR eyes up!' Beth yelled at me.

'Sorry!' I said, but it is hard not to screw your eyes up when your twelve-year-old is coming at you with a mascara wand. I didn't usually let Beth do my make-up but she'd shown me this article in one of her magazines about how to make your eyes look bigger.

'Your eyes *are* a bit small,' she'd said, cocking her head to one side as she looked at me. 'I'll do your eyes for you.'

Several layers of colour later I caught my mum's eye as Beth studied my old and tatty make-up collection. Mum winked at me.

'You haven't got any pink,' Beth said. 'Pink is totally the best colour for bringing out blue eyes, it says here.' She waved the magazine article at me and I looked at the face of the model with her perfectly smooth, blemish-free skin.

'Or making you look like you've got an eye infection,' Mum said, chuckling into her cup of tea.

'It's fashion, Nan,' Beth said, shooting Mum a look over her shoulder. 'You must have had fashion too when you were alive!'

'I'm not dead yet,' my mum said, but she wasn't cross.

'Am I going to look like her,' I said nodding at the model. Beth laughed.

'Don't be mad,' she said. 'She's about sixteen and anyway it's all done on computers now. She's probably got bags under her eyes and loads of spots. Everyone knows that magazine models aren't real.' She turned back to me and surveyed my face. 'You need pink. I think I've got some pink in my room,' she said brightly. 'I'll get it.'

I turned to my mum.

'What's it like,' I asked her, pointing at my face.

'It's like you've had one of those extreme makeovers from off the telly and it's gone really wrong,' Mum said, her voice wobbling with a hidden laugh. I picked up my make-up mirror.

She was right.

'I'll re-do it later,' I said. 'When I get to the pub.'

'What, go out of the house like that?' Mum exclaimed. 'I don't know why you let her do it in the first place,' she said, handing me a cup of tea. 'Sometimes I think she's too bossy for her own good that girl. You shouldn't let her bully you.'

A flash of anger shot across my face.

'She is *not* a bully,' I said sharply.

'No, no. I didn't mean that,' Mum said quickly. 'You know what I mean.'

'I know that she likes to feel involved. She likes to feel a part of it,' I said. 'I would hate her to think I was going out there to find a bloke without her having any say in it.'

Mum sat down at the kitchen table and looked at me. 'You have to do some things just for you,' she said. 'That's what I thought all this computer dating stuff is about.' I stared at the reflection of the kitchen light shimmering in the surface of my cup of tea.

'You think all this is stupid, don't you?' I asked Mum. 'All this dating stuff.' I looked up at Mum's face but her expression did not change.

'I don't think that, love,' she said, carefully. 'I

55

want you to get someone in your life. It's just . . . you haven't always made the right choices, Sam. I just want you to be careful. And so does your father,' she added, because she thought I paid more attention to Dad than her.

I sighed. 'I have been careful, Mum. That's why I've been on my own since Beth was three!' I forced my voice to lower to normal again. 'I need more.'

'I know you do,' Mum said. 'But Internet dating? Can't you just wait to meet someone the normal way?'

'The Internet was Beth's idea,' I reminded her. 'I would never have bothered on my own and I've been waiting nine years to meet someone the "normal" way. There is no normal way.'

Mum tucked one chin into another and looked at me over the rim of her mug. 'God knows you deserve a bit of happiness,' she said, which was the nearest I'd ever get to her approval.

'I've been OK, mostly,' I said, smiling at her.

'Well,' Mum said. 'I'm just saying, what if this bloke you're meeting tonight is a decent one and you turn up looking like Coco the Clown because you don't want to upset your twelve-year-old daughter?'

An image of Brendan flashed before my eyes and I felt the knots in my belly tighten. 'You're right,' I said. 'Pass me a baby wipe.'

By the time Beth had come back from her bedroom I had wiped my face clean and put on my usual make-up but with lipstick this time instead of just clear gloss.

'Mu-um!' she said. 'What are you doing?'

'Well, it was lovely,' I said. 'But your nan and I thought it was too special for tonight. I mean it's only a drink down the pub. I thought I'd just put on a bit of lippy, you know, and some mascara. Like I usually do.' Beth sat down heavily at the table and looked at me.

'You mean you hated it,' she said after a moment.

'I didn't hate it, no . . .' I said, sounding uncertain.

'It's all right,' Beth said. 'It wasn't going how I planned. I need to practise. I'll have a go on Keisha tonight and then if you have a second date, like a posh dinner or something I'll do it then and you can wear a dress.'

'Thanks, love,' I said, feeling let off the hook.

'That's OK,' Beth said. 'But you're not wearing jeans tonight, OK? You have to wear a skirt. That black one you got in the sales. With the split in it. And your boots, OK?'

'Good idea,' I said, nodding.

'Are you going to tell her what to drink, too?' Mum said with an edge of sarcasm.

'Well, not too much for starters,' Beth said seriously. 'You've got work in the morning.'

Mum and I smiled at each other. Maybe Beth *was* a bit bossy but she had this kind of solid certainty about everything in life that made her reassuring to be around. Nothing ever scared her.

'I wonder what he'll be like,' Mum said. She opened her packet of Benson & Hedges and took out a ciggie. She wouldn't light it up in here, because of Beth and my asthma, but she liked to hold one when she was having a cup of tea. Later on, when I'd gone and Beth was in her room with Keisha, she'd go and stand on the balcony and smoke it. She'd have another one after *EastEnders* and another just after I got in, while I told her how the evening went. All on the balcony, no matter what the weather.

'Well, at least we know he won't be married,'

58

Mum said, pressing her lips into a thin line of disapproval.

'Or old,' Beth said. 'Joy wouldn't set you up with an old bloke. Well, not older than you, I mean.'

'Who does Joy know who's a nice catch?' Mum asked, leaning back in her chair holding her fag between her thumb and finger as if she were about to take a deep drag.

We all thought for a long moment. I don't know who they were thinking about but I was thinking about Brendan.

The more I thought about it, the more I thought it *had* to be him. I'm not the sort of person who expects good luck and happiness. In fact, I spend most of every day thinking of all the things that can go wrong, as if thinking of them will somehow stop them from happening. When I was younger I never saw the bad stuff coming and I was never ready for it. So now I try and think of the worst thing. If I'm prepared for it, it won't happen. And I try not to let myself feel too happy, because if I do I'm sure that I'll jinx myself.

But no matter how hard I tried, I couldn't stop thinking that it would be Brendan waiting for me in the bar tonight. I don't know why. I just had this funny feeling in my gut that made me certain that it would be him. I tried to pretend it wasn't there. But it was bubbling away all the time. And I was starting to believe it.

'I hope he's tall,' Beth said. 'There's nothing worse than kissing a man shorter than you are.' I decide not to rise to the bait.

'And clean,' Mum said. 'I hope he's clean with a steady job.'

'And funny,' Beth said. 'A good sense of humour is really sexy in a man.'

'Beth!' Mum and I said together. Beth shrugged.

'Well, it is,' she said, holding up the magazine. 'It says so in here!'

'Well, at least if Joy's arranged it he'll be better than the last bloke you had a date with down the White Horse,' my mum said, deciding to change the subject.

I frowned as it took a second for me to remember who she was talking about. And then it came back.

'Yeah,' Beth said. 'At least this one *should* turn up.'

The One I Didn't Meet At All in the End Because He Never Turned Up

I walked into the bar.

I never usually go down the White Horse during the week but I was glad to see it was almost completely dead. Just a few of the usual regulars stood around the bar including Janet, the butchest woman I have ever seen, with her husband, Frank. Joy said if ever there was somebody with issues it was Janet, but not very loudly because she was as hard as nails and once broke this bloke's arm in two places for calling her a lesbian. And I saw Old Joe sitting in the corner by the fruit machine making his half a pint of Guinness last and chatting to whichever one of his invisible demons he'd brought out with him tonight.

I looked at a few lads standing around one of the pub's tellies watching a game of footy with their arms crossed. It couldn't have been a local team playing because if it was the place would have been packed with fans baying for blood.

I couldn't see my date or anyone who I thought might be him. I didn't have a photo this time so had to go on his very modest description of himself. Average height. Average build. Average looks. The space where it should have been on the website said 'photo pending'. So I just had the description and a name: John Smith.

And he'd said I would know him because he'd be the one drinking half a lager.

'Not a very exciting name,' I'd said to Beth when she'd read out his message to me.

'Don't be an idiot,' she'd said. 'What are you, twelve?' Then she'd realised what she'd said and we'd laughed.

John Smith didn't have an exciting name but I liked the sound of his profile. He didn't sound flashy or like he was trying to impress. He sounded like a normal bloke and his message was sort of funny instead of trying too hard to be interesting. Beth decided I should give him a go. I couldn't believe it when he suggested we meet in the White Horse.

'He must be local,' Beth said.

'Yeah,' I said, feeling suddenly worried. 'But who?'

'He can't know you,' Beth had said. 'Because if he did he would never ask you out.'

I blinked at her.

'On the *Internet*, I mean,' she replied quickly. 'Because if he knew you he'd ask you out face to face!'

I walked up to the bar, but there was no one around. I fished in my pocket for the tenner I'd brought out. Wrapped up inside it was a joke from Beth.

Why are ghosts invisible?
They wear see-through clothes!

Right now *I* felt like I was invisible. Even Old Joe's ghostly drinking pals were getting more attention than me.

Then Brendan came out from the back.

'Hi, Sam,' he said, smiling. I felt my stomach bubble and wished I hadn't rushed my tea. 'Wow, you look great!'

'Thanks,' I said, examining the money in my hand so that my hair fell over my face. 'Um, a glass of wine please?' I asked him from underneath my fringe. He raised an eyebrow.

'Not your usual then?' he asked.

I shook my head. I don't know why, but a Bacardi Breezer didn't seem like the right thing to be drinking on a first date.

'Don't usually see you here on a Tuesday,' Brendan said. 'It's nice to have a pretty face to brighten the place up.' I didn't say anything for a moment but looked at the polished wood of the bar top through the yellow wine. It wobbled and wavered. That was how I felt just then.

'No, well . . .' I paused. For some reason I didn't want to tell Brendan that I was waiting for a date. But I had to because when John Smith turned up he'd know anyway. 'I've got a date,' I said, taking a reluctant sip of the wine. I really didn't like drinking wine much.

I expected Brendan to laugh or be surprised when I told him about my date but his face didn't move.

'Yeah?' he said after a second.

'Yeah,' I said. There was a long time when he seemed like he was going to say something else but then Janet waved her pint glass at him from the other end of the bar. He smiled at me and winked.

'Don't move,' he told me, before going off to serve her. I realised I was hoping that John Smith would not be coming into the bar before Brendan had finished serving Janet.

I looked at the clock behind the bar. It was

gone eight. John Smith was twelve minutes late. That was all right, twelve minutes. That didn't mean anything except traffic, or not being able to find your front door keys. Brendan came back to where I was standing and punched some numbers into the till, before dropping in the coins Janet had given him.

'Thanks for the drink, Jan,' he called out to her. 'I'll take half a lager with you.' I watched him as he poured himself a drink. I noticed he had nice arms.

'You know,' he said in a low voice, as he poured his own drink. 'It takes a special kind of man to love a woman like Janet. I'm not saying she's not a wonderful lady – but, still, that Frank must have balls the size of boulders.' He made me laugh just as I took a mouthful of wine, so I spurted a bit out. I wiped my mouth with the back of my hand and hoped Brendan hadn't noticed me dribble.

'Not here then yet? Your date?' Brendan asked me, looking around the bar.

'No,' I said, with a shrug. 'He's running a bit late, I expect. But I reckon he'll get here. He didn't sound like the arsehole type.'

'No?' Brendan said, smiling. 'I'm glad.' When

65

he was behind the bar the raised floor made him look about two inches taller than me. When he'd come out from behind the bar to collect glasses or something I'd noticed that he was almost exactly the same height as me, so that when he talked to me I was looking straight into his eyes. He was the first person I'd met in my life who had properly green eyes. Not hazel or grey but proper green, like the glass in a beer bottle. He had lovely eyes.

'Do you want another?' Brendan asked me. I looked down. Somehow I had finished my wine. That was probably why my tongue felt numb. I glanced at the clock again, it was nearly half-past eight. John Smith was now half an hour late. That was a broken down car, ran out of petrol or fallen down a lift shaft kind of late.

'I suppose,' I said, glancing over my shoulder and feeling the weight of the change in my pocket. 'I'll have one more and then if he's not here by then . . .'

'Have one more on me,' Brendan said, and he put a bottle of melon-flavoured Bacardi Breezer down in front of me. My favourite drink.

'Thanks,' I said and smiled at him as he put a straw in the top of the bottle. I was pleased he'd remembered what I like to drink. I mean, I knew it was his job to know what his regulars were having, but I was pleased anyway. It's nice to have someone remember something special about you.

'What I don't get,' Brendan said, propping his chin on one elbow as he looked at me. 'Is why you bother with all this Internet stuff? I mean, you're a great-looking woman, Sam. You must get asked out all the time! I see guys looking at you on a Friday night.' I felt the skin across my nose and cheeks begin to heat up again.

'I don't,' I said. 'Joy says I don't give off the right signals. I think it's because they are all looking at Joy, not me. And anyway, even if I did get asked out . . .' I paused. I had no idea how much Brendan knew about me or how much I wanted him to know. 'It's important to me that I don't just end up having a one-night stand.'

'Because of your daughter, you mean?' Brendan asked me.

'Yes,' I said. He knew a bit more than I expected. 'Because of Beth, but also because of me, too. I . . . want something that will be good.'

67

'I know what you mean,' Brendan said. 'So you're saying that you like to get to know a man properly before you get serious. You don't like a guy to just ask you out and see how it goes. You like to make sure he's a decent sort before you get really involved.'

'Yes,' I said, sounding a bit surprised. He *did* know exactly what I meant.

'Me too,' he said, and then his cheeks flushed red. 'With girls I mean.' I laughed again and Brendan laughed too.

'So – how does the Internet help you do that, then?' he asked me. 'Because, you know, I might give it a go, if it's working for you.'

'Well, the person you're meeting . . .' I looked at the clock once more. 'Supposed to be meeting, has to tell you a bit about themselves and you do the same. It's not like pulling some bloke you've just met on a Friday night. You sort of know what you're getting.' I smiled and shrugged. 'At least you're supposed to, but so far it hasn't quite worked out like that for me.'

'I heard.' Brendan looked at me with those green eyes. 'Don't you think that sometimes you should just let your feelings tell you what to do?' he said. Something in his voice made my chest tighten and I reached into my pocket for my inhaler before I realised it was not the early signs of an asthma attack that was making my heart race.

'Um,' I said, looking down at the bar top again. 'Not really.'

I looked around at the still near-empty bar again. 'Well, it looks like this John Smith's not coming.' I said, making myself look up again. 'And I had high hopes for him too.'

'You did?' Brendan asked me.

'Yes,' I said. 'He seemed, you know – nice. Real, like he wasn't pretending to be someone else.' I laughed. 'That's why I don't let my feelings tell me what to do. I'm always wrong!'

'No one is *always* wrong,' Brendan said.

As I pulled my jacket on I looked around the bar, still hopeful that John Smith might turn up after barely escaping from being kidnapped by aliens.

But he still had not arrived by the time I had done up the last button.

'Well, bye then,' I said to Brendan.

'Sam,' he said and he reached out his hand across the bar and caught hold of my fingers. 'Look, I'm really sorry . . . I . . .'

'Why?' I asked him, looking at his fingers holding mine. 'It's not your fault John Smith is an arsehole after all!' He let go and my hand dropped like a stone to my side.

'I'm sorry that he didn't turn up, I mean,' Brendan said, sounding like he really was sorry, before adding quietly, 'And he's a fool, whoever he is.'

'Thanks, Brendan,' I said, suddenly wishing I wasn't about to leave.

'I'm glad he didn't turn up, though,' Brendan said. 'I'm glad we got a chance to talk, just us two, to get to know each other a bit better.'

Before I could reply Janet called him from the other end of the bar, waving her empty pint glass.

'Bye,' I said again, but Brendan was already at the other end of the bar.

When I stepped out of the warm smoky air of the pub into the brisk cold of the night I went back over the evening. I realised I wasn't feeling annoyed or upset that John Smith hadn't turned up. In fact, I was glad that he hadn't turned up.

By the time I stepped out of the lift and let myself into the flat I knew for a fact that I fancied Brendan. And there was this other little nagging thought that kept popping up, too. One that said that, after the way he'd acted and the things he'd said, he might fancy me too. But I didn't let myself think that one too often.

After all, I didn't want to jinx myself.

CHAPTER NINE

'YOU LOOK GREAT, MUM,' Beth said to me as I stood on the doorstep. I tried to move but I could not make my feet walk towards the lift door. I hadn't been this bad on the other three dates. But I hadn't really cared about the other three dates.

'You do look lovely,' Mum said, managing to smile despite the frown slotted between her brows. 'I just hope this one is worth it.'

'I reckon he will be,' Beth said. 'I've got a funny feeling about it, plus your stars said that today you'd have a "pleasant surprise that would change everything".'

Still my feet had not moved.

'Go on then!' Beth said impatiently, giving me a little shove. I tottered onto the smooth surface of the corridor in my heeled boots.

'Bye, then,' Mum said, going back into the flat as the music from *Emmerdale* started up in the front room. 'Have a nice time.'

'I'll walk you to the lift,' Beth said. She hooked her arm through mine as we walked the few steps to the lift and then she pressed the down button.

'It'll be fine,' she said, patting my arm 'Don't be nervous.'

'I am fine,' I said looking at her. 'I might just stay at home.'

The lift doors slid open.

'Don't be stupid,' Beth said, giving me a gentle shove in the right direction. I stepped into the lift and turned round to look at her, my finger holding down the 'doors open' button.

'I love you, Beth,' I said, suddenly needing to tell her. She rolled her eyes.

'Yeah yeah,' she said. 'Go on!'

'OK,' I said, still holding down the 'doors open' button. Beth grinned at me.

'Bye, Mum!' She said pressing the down arrow again.

I took my fingers off the button and the doors slid to a close. I felt the lift begin to move down.

Without Beth I don't think I would have got into the lift.

She is always the one making me take a step

further, keeping me going and making me *live*.

I used to try and imagine, just after Adam had left, what my life would have been like if I hadn't had her so young, but I couldn't. Since the first moment I held her she had been my heartbeat.

It's funny to think that if things hadn't happened the way they did, if I had just kept my head down at school and taken my exams like I was supposed to, then I never would have met Adam. I never would have got pregnant just before I turned sixteen.

But I didn't keep my head down and do my exams.

I fell in love with Luke Goddard instead.

CHAPTER TEN

I WAS *SO* IN LOVE with Luke Goddard. There was something about him that made my insides bubble when I looked at him, he was so confident and dishy. Yes, dishy was the word we used back then. Luke Goddard was a dish.

But I wasn't the only one in love with him. All the girls at school fancied him, and he knew it.

I knew I'd be the last one he'd look at. It didn't stop me dreaming, though. I day-dreamed about it so often that I was so shocked the day he asked me out I had to pinch myself hard.

'Me?' I'd asked him, looking over my shoulder for someone else.

'Yeah,' he said smiling at me. 'You're really pretty. Meet me down the park after school. We'll go for a walk. But don't tell anyone yet, OK? Let's keep it to ourselves for now.'

And I didn't tell anyone I was meeting Luke Goddard, not even Joy, because I was sure that if I went to meet him it was probably just a set-up. I'd turn up at the park and it would be empty or worse, full of his mates jeering and laughing. And Joy would think that, too, so I didn't tell her because I *wanted* it to go well.

Looking back I think I must have read too many of those photo-story comics, the ones where the plain Jane always ends up with the dishy guy at the disco. I kidded myself that happy endings like that happened in real life, too.

When I got to the park and saw that he was sitting on the swings waiting for me, I remember feeling scared by how happy I felt.

'All right?' he said.

'Yeah,' I said.

He stood up.

'Do you want to be my girlfriend?' he said.

'OK,' I said. It wasn't how it went in my magazines, but it was still the most exciting thing anybody had ever said to me.

'Come on, then,' he said. He took my hand and led me towards the back of the park where there was a little bit of woodland. When we got

there I saw that he'd laid out a blanket on top of
the dried leaves. I just looked at it.

'What's that for?' I said.

'Come on,' he said. And he kissed me.

Luke Goddard was a good kisser. I'd never
been kissed before and I didn't know what it
would be like. But the way he kissed me was
lovely. It was a warm evening. I felt the heat of
the setting sun on my cheeks. We kissed for a
long time before anything else happened.

'I've always liked you,' Luke Goddard said,
resting the palm of his hand on my chest. 'Can
I . . .?' he asked me.

I let him because he was gentle and tender
and because I wanted him to. His hands shook
as he unbuttoned my shirt and when I took off
my bra the look on his face made me feel
beautiful.

He asked me if I'd let him do other things and
I did because I was happy. Happy to have Luke
Goddard kissing and touching as we lay on the
blanket in the warmth of the setting sun. He
asked me if I really was his girlfriend. He
sounded worried that I might change my mind.

'I am, I am,' I whispered. He said he wanted
to 'do it' with me and I knew what he meant.

79

He said he'd be really careful and I wouldn't have to worry because no one gets pregnant the first time they do it. He said that he loved me.

I don't think even then I really believed it was true, but I didn't care because I loved him and I loved that moment we were sharing, with the sun on our skin and our arms around each other. I wanted it to happen.

So I said yes.

The sex part was over almost before it started and I don't remember much about it, except that there was a plastic bottle top sticking into the small of my back and every time Luke moved his head the glare of the sun made me close my eyes. But it didn't matter because the sex wasn't important to me. What was so special and what I don't think I have ever felt since, not even when I was happy with Adam, was feeling truly cherished.

Afterwards he rolled off me and pulled me into his arms so that my head was on his chest. I listened to the beat of his heart. I find I sometimes still dream about him in the last few moments before I open my eyes in the morning – Luke on top of me breathing into my hair. And I remember feeling so happy and cared for.

It was that feeling that made everything that happened afterwards so hard to bear.

'Fantastic,' Luke spoke first. We lay like that for a long time until the sun lost its warmth and the sky began to get dark and Luke Goddard helped me pull my clothes back on and walked me home.

'I'll see you tomorrow,' I said, expecting him to kiss me.

'I do really like you, Sam,' he said instead and he went home.

I lay awake all night feeling excited and happy. I really thought that from that moment everything would change because my photo-story had come true. I'd be Luke Goddard's girlfriend and everyone would like me again.

But the next day the fact that I'd slept with Luke Goddard was all round the school.

'Luke Goddard says you fuck for a pound,' Matthew Green said. 'I've got fifty pence – will you do me a blow job?'

'Shut up,' I shouted at him. 'That's not what . . . shut up!' I saw Luke walking towards us.

'Luke,' I said. 'Tell them!'

'Oooh, Luke!' Matt Green and his mates chanted.

'Tell them I'm your girlfriend!' I pleaded. Luke didn't look at me but kept on walking.

'Luke!' I said, feeling my stomach clench. 'Tell them I'm your girlfriend!'

Luke turned around and grinned at me.

'Nice body,' he said. 'Shame about the face.'

It was as if he had slapped me and in a way I wished he had. Because for the rest of that day and the next and all the days left until I turned sixteen and could finally walk out of school, anything would have been better than the lies and rumours that Luke Goddard spread about me. Anything would have been better than having to read what I was supposed to have done with him written on the toilet wall.

What made it even more painful was that I was still in love with Luke. Part of me thought that after what had happened between us he *must* feel the same way about me. He just couldn't say it, so it wasn't really his fault.

So I carried a torch for Luke for the longest time.

In fact, I was still in love with him on the day I met Adam.

CHAPTER ELEVEN

I STOPPED OUTSIDE THE BAR.

Despite the cold air my face felt hot. I stood for a moment beside the door that led into the pub.

I stuffed my fingers into my pockets against the cold and felt a folded piece of paper there. I smiled, took it out and unfolded it, holding it up against the light that shone through the frosted glass door.

Why did the woman who walked into the bar have to go to hospital?
It was an iron bar!

I tried to smile but I couldn't. I shivered and felt like – as my mum would say – someone had just walked over my grave.

I pulled down the hem of my skirt and flicked my hair back off my shoulders.

I walked into the bar.

The first person I saw was Brendan standing behind the bar chatting to the woman he was serving. Smiling and joking with her exactly the way he did with me.

'And a vodka orange for you, of course,' he said to her with a wink. He looked up and saw me.

'Hi, Sam,' he called. But before I could reply I felt an arm slip through mine.

'Hi!' Marie looked excited. She pulled me away from the pub door to the quiet end by the Ladies. Joy was standing there, one leg straight, one leg bent, so that the curve of her hip jutted out at an angle as she leant against the bar. When she saw me she smiled.

'You're looking good, babe,' she said, pushing my jacket off my shoulders and twirling me round. As I turned I saw Brendan, clipping the lids off bottles of Bud before setting them in a line on the bar.

Brendan was working. I wasn't meeting Brendan.

I had begun to believe it so much that it was taking a second for my brain to catch up with my sinking heart.

'So,' I said, feeling suddenly tired and old. 'Let's get on with it.'

'In a minute,' Joy said. She looked at Marie. Marie bit her lip. 'Now listen, you know this man. You haven't seen him for a long time. For a really, really long . . .' I opened my mouth.

'It's not Adam,' Joy said firmly. 'Anyway I saw this bloke the other day on the bus. His car had broken down. *He never normally takes the bus!* When he asked after you I thought it must be like fate, right? It must be meant to be. He said he wanted to see you again. And I want you to know I thought about it for a long time, Sam. Me and Marie talked about it. We thought you should meet. *I* thought you should meet.'

'Meet who?' I said, starting to lose my temper.

Joy put her hand on my shoulder and guided me round the bar to where I could see a man in a suit, his dark head bent over his mobile phone as he sent a text.

'Luke Goddard!' she said.

I felt as if the breath had been sucked out of my lungs. I felt fifteen again with my heart thundering in my chest as I looked at him sitting on the swings waiting for me.

I should have seen this coming. It was

obvious really. But I hadn't thought of it, so I hadn't stopped it.

All I knew was that I didn't want to see Luke Goddard, because the moment I realised that that man was him, all I could feel was the cold hard slap of those insults and lies hitting me in the face again. All I could see was the look of contempt and disgust Luke had given me when I asked him to help me. Everything I thought I had put behind me for good was being raked up again.

I felt angry, humiliated and scared.

And I hadn't felt like that since the night I broke up with Adam.

The One Who Broke my Nose and Three Ribs

He walked in from the bar.

'Dinner's ready,' I said, keeping my eyes down. I knew better than to look at him until I could tell what kind of mood he was in. Sometimes he'd slip his arms around my waist and kiss my ear and I'd know that he was in a good mood.

And when he was happy, he was the Adam I was in love with. Kind and loving. Funny and sweet. I knew that Adam would be gentle with me. He would hold me like I was made of glass. He would make Beth laugh and laugh before reading her a bedtime story. That was the Adam I'd fallen in love with, the Adam I couldn't leave.

But sometimes Adam wasn't like that. Sometimes he got angry, really angry. And the last few times he'd got that angry, he'd hit me.

It went like this. Sometimes he kissed me. Sometimes he would bring me flowers. Sometimes he would do the washing up. And sometimes he'd hit me. But I still loved him and so did Beth. She was three then and she was a proper little daddy's girl.

It had started out as slaps. Slaps became shoves. And then, about a year before that night, he had punched me hard in the stomach. Knocked the wind right out of me. I had bent over double on the kitchen floor and had waited for another breath to come. He had stood in the doorway and watched me. He didn't cry that time. He didn't say he was sorry and that he didn't mean it. He wasn't sweet or

87

loving. He didn't hold me and stroke my hair. He just went out and didn't come back until two days later. That was the first time he punched me, but it wasn't the last.

When I tried to tell Joy how it was, she didn't understand.

'He *hit* you,' she said. 'A guy lays a finger on me and I'm outta there!'

'But that's not really him,' I said. 'Most of the time things are really good.'

'You don't have to put up with a beating to get a few good times, Sam,' Joy had told me. 'If he really loved you he wouldn't touch you. You've got to get out of there. What about Beth?'

'He's a great dad,' I said. 'He loves me.'

'He *loves* you and he's done *that* to you?' Joy winced as she looked at me. 'Get your stuff and come to mine till we sort something out.' But I hadn't listened. I still loved him.

It hadn't always been love. But the first moment I saw him unloading bricks off the back of a lorry for our neighbour's extension I knew that I wanted him. I'd been out of school for less than a month and I was on the way back from the shops with a loaf of bread. It was hot. He had no shirt on. I'd never felt anything like that before. It wasn't love, it was lust. Suddenly I wanted to know what it would be like to press my skin against his. Adam was older than me, nearly twenty-five, so I thought my parents would hate him. But Adam could charm the birds from the trees when he wanted to. They loved him before I did. I knew the exact moment I fell in love with him. It was when I told him I was pregnant. He put his hand on my belly and told me he'd look after me and never leave me. That was the moment I started loving him.

Nothing in my life had ever been as good as those first few years in that flat with Adam and Beth. I felt like a real person at last with my own family. I felt happy and safe. I couldn't let that go without trying to get it back. So when he came in from the pub I kept my head down and hoped for the best.

'Where's Beth?' he asked, his voice short and dark. Every part of me tensed.

'In bed,' I said keeping my voice light. 'Has been for hours! Your tea's ready. Do you want a lager with it?'

'Why are you having a go at me?' he shouted. Just like that. He exploded, knocking the dishes

I had set out on the table onto the floor. 'Nag, nag, nag! That's all you ever do!'

He was right up in my face then. His angry mouth stretched into a snarl, the stink of stale beer on his breath. I leant back away from him and I could feel the edge of the worktop bite into my spine.

'I'm not,' I said, even though I knew saying anything was the wrong thing to do. Part of me still hoped that the other Adam, the Adam I loved, might hear my voice and remember he loved me. 'I just said your tea was ready.'

I smiled at him.

He slammed the back of his fist into the right side of my head. I went down. He kicked me hard in the ribs twice with his boots, making me cough the air out of my lungs. I remember I could see under the fridge. I remember thinking it really needed cleaning. I could hear Beth's thin cry rise above the whirr and rattle of the washing machine.

I wasn't going to do anything else then. I was just going to wait for it to be over, wait for Adam to finish and go to bed so that I could go to Beth and get her back off to sleep like I had done before.

But then Adam did something different.

He crouched down beside me.

'Can't you hear your kid crying? Someone like you shouldn't be allowed to have kids,' he said, his voice quiet, almost a whisper. 'Someone like you isn't fit to be a mother. I should never have touched you, you dumb fucking whore. You tricked me into getting you pregnant.' He spat the words in my face. 'Someone's got to bring that kid up right. Someone's got to bring her into line so she doesn't grow up into a slag like you.' He stood up and looked down the hallway.

'I'll show her,' he said and he walked out of the kitchen.

I don't know how but I was on my feet. Every breath I took felt like fire was spreading over my chest and I could taste my blood in my mouth. I knew whatever happened, whatever he did to me, he wasn't going to lay a finger on Beth.

That was the moment when I stopped loving him.

'No!' I managed to scream. He had opened her door and she was sitting up in bed holding her teddy to her chest. She had stopped crying.

The tears stood in her bright eyes. I could feel her fear.

I lunged at him. I jumped on his back and pulled him off balance. He slammed me into the hall wall. I felt something else crack.

He turned around and looked at me. There was nothing left in his eyes of the Adam I had still loved right up until the moment he threatened my daughter. There was nothing left in his face at all except hate.

A loud knock rattled the glass in the front door.

'What's going on in there?' It was Mr Radcliff, the old man from next door. 'I'm warning you, I'm calling the police!' His voice was shaking. He was afraid but he kept knocking on the front door.

I looked at Adam and waited as he drew back his fist.

The next punch broke my nose.

I expected him to go for me again. But instead he headed for the front door and flung it open. Mr Radcliff wasn't there, but I could hear sirens growing louder. Adam looked at me one last time and walked out.

I never saw him again. I didn't even press

charges, although the police really wanted me to. I couldn't face it. I moved back home with Mum and Dad and he hung around for a while trying to get back into my life but I didn't see him. I didn't go out at all and there was always someone at home with me. After a couple of months my brother and three of his mates met him one night as he was leaving the pub. They persuaded him he should move on. I heard he went to London.

Sometimes I try to think about the first few years that Adam and I were together. I try to think about the good times, like when he'd made me and Beth a surprise picnic for Beth's first birthday. But I can't. All I can think about is that the last man I loved broke my nose and three ribs.

And I think there must be something really wrong with me.

CHAPTER TWELVE

'GET OUT OF MY way,' I said, and pushed Joy to one side as I headed towards the pub doors.

'What?' Joy stepped in front of me again. 'Why? Where are you going?' She asked me, looking surprised. I shook my head as I looked at her. I couldn't believe that she didn't know why I was so angry.

'I thought I was going on a date with . . .' I stopped myself saying Brendan's name. 'Luke Goddard!' I shook my head in disbelief. 'Joy, you of all people should know what he did to me! He made my life hell. He made me think that someone like Adam was my knight in shining armour!' I pushed past Joy again and got two steps further before she stopped me.

'Sam, wait!' She held the top of my arm. 'Please. Just listen to me for a second.'

I pulled her fingers loose and waited.

'OK,' she said. 'We were stupid. We should have told you from the start who you were meeting. But we didn't think you'd come if you knew!'

'Actually that part was Joy's idea,' Marie said.

'Marie!' Joy exclaimed. 'You're not helping.'

Marie shrugged.

'Too bloody right I wouldn't have come,' I hissed at them both, trying hard not to attract attention. 'And now I'm going home. Get out of my way.'

But Joy didn't move.

'You told me once you still thought about Luke Goddard and how different things might have been.'

I stared at her in disbelief.

'I didn't!' I said.

'You did,' she said. 'That's why I thought . . .'

'If I said that, I was drunk or brain damaged or *something*. I don't even remember saying it.' I shook my head. I couldn't believe her.

Joy lowered her voice as a few people looked over our way. Even the greatest hits CD that Brendan had turned up to full volume couldn't disguise the fact that something was going on with us.

96

'Sam, babe – if you could just talk to him, then . . .'

'I can't believe you'd think . . .' I began, hearing my voice roll like low thunder.

'Just hear me out,' Joy held up the palm of her hand. 'You never knew, did you? You never knew if he really liked you, or if he'd meant the whole thing as a sick wind up right from the start. Well, now you can ask him.' Joy's voice softened. 'Look, he seemed to me like he really wanted to see you. To set things straight. Don't you want that too? To finally move on . . .'

'That's what I've been trying to do,' I said. 'What I thought I had done until you raked all this up. Luke Goddard? Joy, why? You must be sick!'

'I just thought,' Joy kept talking. 'Well, I've seen it on the telly. You know, when they get people to confront their painful past. It helps them to find a new strength to live their lives with.' Joy put a hand on my shoulder. It felt heavy. I shrugged it off. 'If you talk to Luke, you could tell him how he made you feel. You could make him see what he did and how it's affected you since.'

Joy glanced through the crowd of Friday-night drinkers and I caught a glimpse of Luke fiddling nervously with his mobile. 'I think he really regrets it. I think if you talk to him you'll feel better. You'll see he's no better than you.'

'I know that,' I said sharply.

'Do you?' Joy asked me. 'Do you really?'

At that moment I hated her but there was some truth in what Joy said. Since that afternoon in the park there had been a lot of times when I'd wondered if all the things I'd felt had been in my imagination alone, if I had really been that stupid. I did want to know.

'I'll talk to him,' I said to Joy.

'You won't regret it,' Joy said, smiling with relief.

'No,' I said, shooting her an angry look. 'But you will.'

CHAPTER THIRTEEN

'LUKE,' I SAID. I SAT down and made myself look at him. The first thing I noticed about him was that he was losing his hair.

'Sam!' He smiled, and looked nervous. 'You look exactly the same. You look great, really great. Can I get you anything, a drink or anything?'

I shook my head and watched Luke's mouth open and close twice before any more words came out.

'I'm so glad you've come,' he said.

'Why are we here, Luke?' I asked him. I didn't want to make small talk.

'I thought Joy told you . . .' he began, looking anxious.

'Joy told me I was going on a date,' I said.

Luke said nothing for a second and then he said, 'I've been thinking about you a lot, Sam,' he said. For a second my eyes drifted over his head and I could see Brendan behind the bar flirting with a group of girls just a few years older than Beth. I made myself look at Luke again.

'Have you?' I said. Every moment that I was near him I could feel a cold hard ball of anger growing and tightening in my chest, making it harder to breathe. I wanted to reach for my inhaler but I was worried it would make me look weak.

'The way I treated you after . . . I'm really sorry.'

I bit my lip hard until it hurt.

'One two! One two!' The voice of the DJ setting up the Friday-night disco boomed out across the background noise of music and voices.

'You're sorry?' I asked him. It didn't sound like I wanted it to. It sounded as if I was surprised that he should be sorry. Almost grateful.

Luke smiled at me, a shadow of his old smile.

'I am,' he said. 'I really am. And I want you to know that that afternoon with you – it meant a lot to me. I really did like you. I really did want to go out with you. I had done for ages. All the boys fancied you, but none of them would go near you because . . . well, it wasn't cool. I didn't care about that, though. I didn't care about what the others would say . . .'

I heard myself laugh sharply.

'Funny that,' I said. 'Because that's not exactly how I remember it.' My voice was stronger now. It sounded more like how I felt inside.

Luke bowed his head and I could see his pink scalp shining through his thinning hair.

'I'm saying that that's what I wanted to do but . . . I wasn't strong enough,' he said, looking up at me at last.

'So you didn't want to go out with me,' I said. 'I expected that. I could have got over it. But why did you have to turn my life into a living hell? Why did you say all that stuff about me, Luke? What did I ever do to you?'

Luke could not look me in the eye.

'Nothing,' he said. 'But I had to do it, Sam. If I didn't they would have laid into me! You know how kids are.'

I said nothing. I couldn't find a way to respond to that. To Luke Goddard sweeping away the years of pain and hurt he'd put me

101

through as if it was something . . . ordinary. Something to be expected. My silence seemed to encourage him.

'Sam, the thing is,' he said. 'I've got kids now. Two girls, Katy and Martha. If the same thing happened to them . . .' Luke shook his head. 'I don't know what I'd do. I've come here tonight to ask you . . . Will you forgive me, Sam?'

It felt as if time had frozen for a second. All I could hear was the blood pounding in my ears as I thought about what Luke Goddard had just asked me. At that moment all I wanted was for it to be over. For him to be gone and for me to be free to go home and be with my family again. To turn the TV up loud and shut out the world.

'Whatever,' I said flatly, pressing my anger out of my voice, lifting and dropping my shoulders in a shrug. I'd say anything for this to be over. It wasn't me moving on. It was just raking up a past I tried every day to forget.

But Luke didn't seem to understand that – he looked as if he thought I really had forgiven him, breathing out a long sigh of relief.

'Thank you,' he said, reaching out for my hand. 'You don't know how much better that makes me feel. Now I can put all that business behind me and move on.'

I snatched my hand out from underneath his as the noise of the pub flooded back in all around me. I thought I was going to let this go for the sake of a quiet life – but I couldn't believe what he had just said.

'You can move on, can you?' I shouted at him as I stood up. People stopped talking and stared at me. 'What about me, Luke? What about me? When do I get to move on? When do I stop waking up in the middle of the night crying because I've been dreaming about what you did to me? When do I stop worrying every second that the same thing is going to happen to my little girl? When do I finally get to put you and all those other sad stupid fucks out of my life for good and move on?' I picked up the pint he'd been drinking. 'I don't forgive you,' I told him coldly. 'I hate you.'

I threw Luke Goddard's pint in his face.

I did that. I couldn't believe it was me but it was. I even think I heard the locals cheering me on.

Luke was shocked for a split second and then he lunged at me and tried to grab me.

'You stupid cow,' he shouted at me.

I pushed him hard, harder than I knew I could and he fell backwards over his chair and onto the floor.

'Don't you ever touch me,' I told him. 'You can never touch me again.'

Suddenly Brendan was there, standing between me and Luke.

'Call the police,' Luke told Brendan. 'I want her charged with assault.'

Brendan did not move.

'Get out,' he said. He sounded friendly and calm but you knew he meant it. 'Get out, now.'

'But . . .' Luke looked at Brendan's face and got up. He picked up his jacket and his phone and turned to say something else to me. Brendan took a step towards him and Luke thought better of it. He was gone.

'Are you OK?' Brendan asked me as the crowds of drinkers closed around Luke's retreating back.

'Fine,' I said and ran into the Ladies' loos.

'Well?' Joy rushed in after me as I ran my hands under the cold tap. 'How did it go?'

I looked at her.

'Get away from me!' I told her angrily, my

voice echoing off the tiles. 'I trusted you more than anyone!'

Joy took a step back.

'Sam, please!' she said, holding the palms of her hands up, 'I'm sorry, I was stupid making up that date stuff. A total plank. But did I get it all wrong?'

I rubbed the blurred make-up from around my eyes. I was still shaking, still furious but I also felt an incredible high.

'Did you actually see any of what happened out there?' I asked Joy. 'I nearly got into a fight because of you! Jesus, Joy, you just dumped me in a great big pile of shit and thought you were doing me a favour.'

'When you put it like that . . .' Joy said, looking worried. 'Look I fucked up but I did see you. You gave him what for! You were brilliant!'

'Was I?' I said. 'Because I didn't think I was like that. I think what I just did to Luke makes me into a bastard like him.'

Joy said nothing for a moment.

'It doesn't,' she said, taking a step closer and putting her arm around me. 'It makes you a strong woman who is not going to lie down for anyone to walk all over her ever again. Do you understand? You're worth a million times what Luke, or Adam or any of those losers that hurt you are. Christ, Sam, I've known that for years. You must know it now, don't you?'

I laid my forehead on Joy's shoulder for a second before I looked up at her.

'I think I do,' I said. 'I really think I do.'

'I should never have built you up with the whole date thing. When I saw Luke and I thought about how he'd hurt you, I thought this was a chance for you to confront him. To have your say and move on. I should have been straight with you from the start but I got carried away as usual. Do you hate me?' Joy asked.

I shook my head.

'No, I don't hate you,' I said. 'I don't hate anyone any more.'

'Next time,' Joy said. 'I promise you that I'm going to set you up on a real blind date.'

I thought of Brendan leaning across the bar flirting with those pretty girls.

'No,' I said. 'No, I'm not doing any more blind dates.'

'What?' Joy looked disappointed.

'You were right,' I said. 'I was only doing it because Beth wanted me to. But I'm happy as I am. I don't need a man to be happy.'

'Really?' Joy asked.

'Really,' I said more firmly than I felt as I looked in the mirror and put on some lippy. The way I felt about Brendan hadn't changed but nobody else needed to know that. I'd just keep it to myself and wait for all of those feelings to fade away.

'I'm giving up men for good.'

The One Who Told Me Something Really Funny

I walked up to the bar and waited to be served.

Joy and Marie were dancing on the makeshift dance floor.

Joy was dancing as close as she could to Sean Jerome, who she had had her eye on for ages. Marie just stood there swaying from side to side getting to that point in the evening when she got all teary and started missing her husband. I knew that in the next ten minutes she would go to the payphone by the Ladies and ring and ask him to come and get her. I don't know why Marie used a payphone because she had a mobile. But she always seemed to forget this when she was drunk.

I watched the bar staff as I waited to be served, too busy to notice me waiting. Even though I really wanted my first drink of the night I didn't mind. I was praying that anyone except Brendan would serve me. I thought it would be all right as he was at the other end of the bar busy with a large round for the pub football team.

'Oi, Brendan mate!' Sean Jerome appeared beside me and shouted down the bar. 'We're dying of thirst down here!'

Brendan looked up and past Sean. He saw me waiting and bent over to whisper something into the ear of one of the barmaids. He smiled at me as he walked towards me.

'I'm on a break,' he told Sean. 'Annie will be with you next, OK?'

He leant over the bar towards me.

'Will you have a drink with me, Sam?' he asked me.

I nodded.

He put an open bottle of melon-flavoured Bacardi Breezer on the bar.

'You don't have to buy me . . .' I began.

'I want to,' he said. 'You deserve it after all that.' He poured himself a pint and set it on the bar top next to my drink. He came out from behind the bar and stood next to me.

'It's loud in here,' he said, leaning forward so that his lips were close to my ear. I could feel the breath his words made.

Brendan looked at me for a moment and took a sip of his drink. The flashing coloured lights from the disco turned him pink, green, yellow and blue in turn.

'Are you OK now?' he asked. 'Tell me to butt out if you like, but I don't think that feller was the one for you. I was getting worried about you but you handled him all right.' He puffed out a breath. 'You were really cool, much harder than me!'

I couldn't help but smile. Knowing that Brendan had managed to notice me while four or five younger girls were throwing themselves at him made me happy.

'Yeah, I am OK,' I said. 'You know how when you build something up in your mind and it gets to be so big that you think you'll never get over it, and then something happens, like a pin bursting a balloon, and the thing that was worrying you has suddenly gone and you don't know why you let it bother you for so long in the first place?'

Brendan frowned and smiled at the same time.

'No, to be honest,' he said. I laughed and thought for a moment.

'Seeing him made me realise that I'm not the person I thought I was. I'm stronger than I thought and happier than I realised. The past isn't as important as I thought it was because I had already moved on and grown up – without even realising it. Funny really,' I said. I sounded much calmer than I felt, but all I wanted right then was a Bacardi Breezer and to talk to Brendan. The sound of his voice made me feel happy.

'I'm glad for you, Sam,' Brendan said. 'You deserve to be happy.'

We watched the dance floor for a second. Joy had wound her arms around Sean's neck and looked like she was hoping to pin him to the nearest wall with her tongue.

'Do you want to hear something really funny?' he said.

I looked into his green eyes.

'Go on,' I said smiling.

'You know when you came in the other night to meet John Smith?'

'That's not funny,' I said, even though it was.

'No,' Brendan took a deep breath. 'What's funny is that I was John Smith.'

I blinked at him. Even with him standing so close the music was too loud because I thought he'd said . . .

'What?' I asked him.

'I was John Smith,' he said again. He really had said it.

'Joy told me you were using this dating web-site and I thought . . . Well, I've been meaning to ask you out for a while now. I asked Joy if she thought you'd go for it. She said you only went out with fellers off this website. We've got a computer out the back so I logged on one day. Saw your photo and details and . . . well, I registered. But then I thought that if you saw my name you'd think I was a real weirdo for not asking you out face to face.' Brendan looked at his boots before looking up again at me. 'So I named myself after a pint of bitter.

'I've got to be honest, Sam. I didn't think it through. By the time you turned up that night

I knew that if I told you John Smith was me I would have blown it for good.'

I stared at him. I couldn't believe what he was telling me. I should have been cross but I felt just the opposite. I felt like laughing.

'Why are you telling me now, then?' I asked.

Brendan thought for a moment.

'Because, even if it makes you hate me I didn't want you to think you'd been stood up,' he said. 'Like I said, I want you to be happy.'

He stood a step closer until his forearm was touching mine.

'Look,' he said. 'I know how to flirt with girls – it's part of my job. But when it comes to asking a woman I really like out, I'm terrible. I always mess it up and say the wrong thing.' He put his pint down and I thought he was about to pick up my hand but he didn't. 'I really like you, Sam, and you probably think I'm some kind of psycho now – but before I told you about John Smith – I thought you might like me too? You were always eyeing me up,' he joked gently.

'I was not!' I protested, laughing.

'No? Damn it,' Brendan said, with a wry smile. 'I've got it wrong *again*.'

I looked at him. He was joking but he looked so worried and sweet.

'You haven't,' I said, and the smile he gave me made me hold my breath.

'Every time I've seen you walk into the bar since the first time, I've wanted to tell you I like you,' he said, dipping his head so that it was closer to mine. 'You go around meeting these losers, telling the whole pub about it as if it's one great big joke and I've been wanting to ask you out, but kept thinking what if I'm the next big joke?'

'You are quite funny,' I said. I was so happy I couldn't stop smiling like an idiot.

'I just can't stand seeing you go through more crap. It's been killing me,' he said. 'So I'm asking you face to face, right now, whether you think I'm funny or not. Would you come out for a drink with me on my night off, Sam? Not here – somewhere quiet where we can talk. Will you go on a date with me? There, I've said it.'

For the second time that night it was like someone had turned down the volume on the whole room. I couldn't hear anything except my heart beating in my ears and then I realised that I was laughing.

'Um,' I said, pretending to think about it.

'Sam!' Brendan protested.

'I will! I will,' I said, and then more quietly, 'Of course I will. It's just that this is so funny.'

'Why?' he said.

I stopped laughing.

'Because I like you too,' I said. 'I have for ages.'

Brendan and I looked at each other for a second longer, as if we had only just met for the first time. He picked up my hand and I felt the warmth of his fingers holding mine.

'Can I kiss you now, then?' he asked me.

I didn't answer him, I just took a step forward and kissed him. I put my arms around his neck and felt his palms on my waist and kissed him. I think some of the bar staff cheered.

When we stopped kissing, Brendan looked at me.

'You're a great woman, you know,' he said. 'Fantastic.'

'Thank you,' I said. When he said it, it felt true.

'I don't want to stop looking at you, or touching you or kissing you,' he said, his voice low and smiling. 'But I've got to go back to work. Please say I can walk you home later?' He held my gaze, looking right into my eyes, and I thought there could be nothing nicer in the world than walking home with Brendan holding my hand, talking and joking, making me laugh and stopping to kiss me every few minutes. Because I somehow knew that was exactly how it was going to be with him.

'You can,' I said, smiling as I watched him go back behind the bar without taking his eyes off me.

Joy and Marie rushed up to me and threw their arms around my neck.

'You dark horse!' Marie said.

'Yeah, and anyway,' Joy said, pretending to be serious. 'You just told me that you were giving up men for good!'

I looked at her and shrugged.

'Don't be silly,' I said. 'I was only joking.'

WORLD BOOK DAY

Quick Reads

We would like to thank all our partners in the *Quick* Reads project for all their help and support:

BBC RaW
Department for Education and Skills
Trades Union Congress
The Vital Link
The Reading Agency
National Literacy Trust

Quick Reads would also like to thank the Arts Council England and National Book Tokens for their sponsorship.

We would also like to thank the following companies for providing their services free of charge: SX Composing for typesetting all the titles; Icon Reproduction for text reproduction; Norske Skog, Stora Enso, PMS and Iggusend for paper/board supplies; Mackays of Chatham, Cox and Wyman, Bookmarque, White Quill Press, Concise, Norhaven and GGP for the printing.

www.worldbookday.com

Quick Reads

BOOKS IN THE *Quick* Reads SERIES

The Book Boy	Joanna Trollope
Blackwater	Conn Iggulden
Chickenfeed	Minette Walters
Don't Make Me Laugh	Patrick Augustus
Hell Island	Matthew Reilly
How to Change Your Life in 7 Steps	John Bird
Screw It, Let's Do It	Richard Branson
Someone Like Me	Tom Holt
Star Sullivan	Maeve Binchy
The Team	Mick Dennis
The Thief	Ruth Rendell
Woman Walks into a Bar	Rowan Coleman

AND IN MAY 2006

Cleanskin	Val McDermid
Danny Wallace and the Centre of the Universe	Danny Wallace
Desert Claw	Damien Lewis
The Dying Wish	Courttia Newland
The Grey Man	Andy McNab
I Am a Dalek	Gareth Roberts
I Love Football	Hunter Davies
The Name You Once Gave Me	Mike Phillips
The Poison in the Blood	Tom Holland
Winner Takes All	John Francome

Look out for more titles in the *Quick* Reads series in 2007.

www.worldbookday.com

Have you enjoyed reading this
Quick Reads book?

Would you like to read more?

Or learn how to write fantastically?

If so, you might like to attend a course to
develop your skills.

Courses are **free** and available in your local area.

If you'd like to find out more,
phone **0800 100 900**.

You can also ask for a **free video or DVD** showing
other people who have been on our courses and
the changes they have made in their lives.

Don't get by – get on.

FIRST CHOICE BOOKS

If you enjoyed this book, you'll find more great reads on www.firstchoicebooks.org.uk. First Choice Books allows you to search by type of book, author and title. So, whether you're looking for romance, sport, humour or whatever turns you on — you'll be able to find other books you'll enjoy.

You can also borrow books from your local library. If you tell them what you've enjoyed, they can recommend other good reads they think you will like.

First Choice is part of The Vital Link, promoting reading for pleasure. To find out more about The Vital Link visit www.vitallink.org.uk

RaW

Find out what the BBC's RaW (Reading and Writing) campaign has to offer at www.bbc.co.uk/raw

NEW ISLAND

New Island publishers have produced four series of books in its Open Door series – brilliant short novels for adults from the cream of Irish writers. Visit www.newisland.ie and go to the Open Door section.

SANDSTONE PRESS

In the Sandstone Vista Series, Sandstone Press Ltd publish quality contemporary fiction and non-fiction books. The full list can be found at their website www.sandstonepress.com.

Quick Reads

The Thief
by Ruth Rendell

Arrow

**What you do in childhood may come back
to haunt you . . .**

Stealing things from people who had upset her
was something Polly did quite a lot.

There was her Aunt Pauline; a girl at school; a
boyfriend who left her. And there was the man
on the plane . . .

Humiliated and scared, by a total stranger, Polly
does what she always does. She steals something. But she never could have imagined that
her desire for revenge would have such terrify-
ing results.

'Ruth Rendell knows how to make your hair
stand up straight on your head'
Maeve Binchy

Quick Reads

Danny Wallace and the Centre of the Universe by **Danny Wallace**

Ebury, May 2006

Danny Wallace wanted to write about the Centre of the Universe, but how was he to get there? And what would he say about it when he did?

Luckily, in a small street in a small town in Idaho a manhole cover had just been declared the Centre of the Universe by the mayor. The science backed his decision and the town rejoiced.

And the name of the town? Wallace. It was a cosmic coincidence Danny couldn't resist . . .

Quick Reads

How to Change Your Life in 7 Steps
by John Bird

Vermilion

Want to improve your life but don't know where to start? Then this is the book for you.

John Bird explains his seven simple rules that could change your life. You might want to get a new job, stop smoking or go back to college. This book tells you how you can take what you've been given and turn it into something you'll be proud of.